The Last Time

An Anthology

ISBN: 978-1-9163441-0-5

This book has been published in the United
Kingdom, therefore any American spellings
originally evident in any poems or stories have
been converted to British, with permission from
the author(s).

DEDICATION

To everyone who has experienced a 'last time' and to those
who have yet to do so – this one's for you!

CONTENTS

ACKNOWLEDGMENTS

Many thanks to all who have contributed to this small, but perfectly formed, anthology. This has been a labour of love for us here at Black Dream. The Last Time is a collection of truly personal poems and stories, and to say it's been an honour to put them together in such a way is quite the understatement. Let us not forget our families and our friends who have provided inspiration, patience, and most importantly, love.
Where would we be without them?

FOREST FIRE

Brad Medd

Forest fire
Home fire
Blistering heat
Beneath my feet
No reason to weep
It won't save you

Forest fire
Home fire
Roars in my face
An utter disgrace
Is all over this place
There's no hiding

Forest fire
Home fire
Through ash and smoke
I crawl and we choke
Too much is broke
Who will fix it

THE LAST TIME

Forest fire
Home fire
Gone as it came
Shot through with pain
Where is the blame
Where is your shame
Nothing is the same
And it never will be.

Brad Medd is an aspiring poet and short story writer from West Yorkshire.

2

PHOTOGRAPH

Paul B. Morris

My sleep is disturbed once more by the sound of a child laughing as she runs across the landing that leads to the bedrooms. I know that the child is a girl and she is lost between worlds. The harmony of her laugh is sweet, innocent, and everything a happy child should sing about. Sadly, the child is far from happy and no words of comfort offered forth will soothe her mood. She is angry with me. She is always so angry, and it breaks my heart.

The child launches herself towards me. Her face is a cold, greyish blue, twisted with angry bloodied scars, eyes rolled back into the recess of her skull. Her small cold fingers clutch the side of my head before she begins to scratch deeply into my skin, tearing sharp lines of pain downwards from my ears to my mouth. Her blind eyes stare at me, her mouth stretches wide into an unpleasant clown-like grin, and drool drops from her lower lip into my terrified mouth which adds to her amusement. She begins to laugh before working her hands further into my open mouth, filling it and leaving me struggling for breath. When she finally speaks, her voice destroys me.

"You weren't watching were you Daddy? YOU WEREN'T WATCHING ME!"

Then, she proceeds to rip my mouth wide open until she has detached my jaw from my skull. As death beckons me forth, she smiles with satisfaction.

I wake from the nightmare once more, massaging my jaw, needing to satisfy myself that I am in one piece. I know the dreams aren't real, I've been through them so many times before. Yet, every time they feel so much more real. As if I am wanting to be slain by the beast. Not that I'd ever call my daughter a monster, especially now that she's no longer with us. I did under more jovial circumstances, mainly when she'd done something rude such as fart and burp, or suck on the worms that had been freshly foraged from the garden as if they were spaghetti. She was often 'Daddy's Little Monster' and I loved her dearly. Now, it's so heart-breaking to see her in the form of a truly terrifying monster that wouldn't be out of place in a gory horror film.

You're not really taught anything as a parent, other than the basics when you're in the maternity ward nervously holding the delicate new-born child in your hands. Sure, you get some advice on how best to feed and clothe them, how to stimulate their fledgling mind, and the safest way for them to sleep in a cot or basket. Essentially, it's all practical instruction that you naturally learn as you go along when you are faced with the reality of raising a tiny human.

Despite being an unconventional couple, Rachel and I had done pretty damn well in the early moments of Libby's life and were proud parents. We listened to most of the advice shared by friends who believed they knew more than we did because they'd had kids. Even my parents chipped in with the odd suggestion, stating that I'd not turned out too bad. We tried to take it all in good spirit, but we ended up doing our own thing. It was actually pretty good when everything was going well. The biggest bastard problem with life and advice is, no one really knows how to deal with the death of a child. Especially when one is taken from you when they're only five years old. Nobody knows or teaches you how to deal with it. Because you can't deal with it. No one can. It's an indescribable pain, mixed together with an overwhelming sensation of guilt. No parent should ever have to experience it. We're meant to watch our children grow whilst they embrace their own world, supporting and nurturing them throughout their journey.

I'd always maintained that I would be a 'Super Daddy' and wouldn't allow anything to happen to my Princess Libby. Even though her name was officially registered as Elizabeth, in memory of Rachel's Grandmother, I always called her Libby. I didn't really want to associate my beautiful daughter with one of Rachel's most foul relatives. A woman who was a stoic disciple of pain and heartless gestures of false love. I have to say that Rachel's mother, Sandra, hadn't fared much better and was considerably devoid of emotional context.

Sadly, Rachel had fallen foul of the family curse and offered little in the way of a loving disposition. Perhaps they hid their emotions somewhere deep so they wouldn't ever be hurt by those who tampered with them? I didn't believe this, to be honest, and simply arrived at the conclusion that they were all miserable arseholes who were unable to open-up their emotions and embrace love. There may have been a back story attached to their perpetual unhappiness and I kind of hoped that I would one day get to hear about it. Maybe then, I could understand Rachel and possibly her mother.

Yet, there was no way through Rachel's armour. Despite my efforts, I couldn't find a chink that would let me in and nearer to her heart. Irrespective of how many times we had sex, there wasn't any love embodied in the act. No tenderness or excitement. It simply became an animalistic function that required output of procreation. I found no enjoyment from the soulless missionary sex that was offered. All Rachel was bothered about was making sure I made her pregnant. It wasn't too long before conception occurred and despite my deep-rooted doubt, I genuinely felt a sense of optimism and hope. Love would always have to take a back seat between us, but I vowed that this would be offered in abundance to our child.

I don't know why I'd first been attracted to Rachel or why we'd entered into a relationship. I guess it had something to do with the fact we were both lonely. Despite not actually loving Rachel, we did seem to get along. Even though I didn't find her particularly attractive and she generally appeared to be devoid of emotion, there was something that clicked between us, although I'm not sure what it was. I knew that it wasn't love though. We'd not been together for very long before Rachel began to talk about wanting children. Initially, I thought our odd relationship was a terrible basis to bring a child into the world. For a start, we weren't in love with each other. Plus, at that time, I wasn't sure that I wanted to remain with Rachel, let alone start a family. Yet, I couldn't walk away from her because selfishly, I didn't want to be lonely. The more and more Rachel spoke about how nice it could be to have a child and how she'd always wanted to be a mother, I slowly began to think that it might not be too bad. Maybe, having a child together would unite us? In many ways, it did. Thirteen months later, on Saturday 28th April 1990 at 15:05 pm, Elizabeth "Libby" Koster was born, weighing 7lb 3oz. At that precise moment, we found a sense of love together.

It's hard to actually pin-point the accident that took Libby from us. Sometimes, I really don't want to acknowledge what happened, because it's too painful and I've almost blanked it from my mind. Not that I want to ignore the loss, far from it. I want to see it played out in my mind on a frequent basis so that I can feel the cut so deeply. I want the visions to hurt me because it's what I deserve. I can feel the icy grip of demons placing their bony hands on my shoulder, teasing me with their false hopefulness. They begin to scratch through my t-shirt, and I tell them to leave me alone but, they don't listen as they continue to molest my body. It finally ends once I screw my eyes shut and think of something happy, which is the final moment I'm with Libby.

It was supposed to be such a beautiful day. It was only one week after Libby's birthday and she desperately wanted to test the new scooter she'd received from Nanny and Granddad Koster. It was garishly pink and was adorned with princess transfers. Everything that Libby disliked in general. She desperately wanted a scooter though and irrespective of my offer to remove the transfers, she simply wanted to ride it. She was incredibly excited, bouncing around the living room, eager for us to take her to the park so that she could ride. I'd told her that it was too dangerous for her to ride the scooter in the street because of the inconsiderate people who lived near to us. Ironically, I'd only meant it as some thinly veiled warning. We busied ourselves and made it outside to the drive, ready to jump into the car. I'd already opened the gates that secured our driveway and watched as Libby ran around the vehicle. I shouted out to her, delivering instructions that she should calm down, move away from the road and get in the car right now. I glanced across to her mother who was transfixed with her phone, no doubt engrossed with whatever issue had now become pertinent among her friends. I disappeared back inside the house to retrieve my wallet, silently cursing Rachel's ignorance under my breath, wishing that she could be a better mother to our daughter whilst acknowledging that I needed to improve as a dad.

The sound of a car desperately trying to brake and come to a halt before it hit Libby full-on, mixed with Rachel's petrified shriek, will forever haunt me. I can never un-hear what I heard, in the same way, I cannot un-see it. I ran from the kitchen, out through the front door, to witness the battered body of my daughter descend heavily to the tarmac in front of a stationary car. What proceeded before us at that time, did so in muted silence. I sprinted forward to the prostrate body of my little angel, knowing that people were screaming and shouting. I pushed past the driver of the car, who'd launched himself free from the driver's seat. He was frantically trying to explain himself, but I didn't care, shoving him aside so that I could cradle my child. I didn't even want her mother anywhere near. Libby lay perfectly still on the cold black road; her face had already become devoid of life. Angry facial wounds began to calm down, clotting together for a final moment in life. My daughter, my angel, was dead, and I knew it.

I frequently look at the photograph on my phone that Rachel had taken of me and Libby posing together with her pink scooter. It was a beautiful shot that captured the love between father and daughter, and I love it so much. A constant reminder of the last time we would ever be together.

Paul B. Morris is a writer who hails from Walsall in the West Midlands, although he was created somewhere up North.

His stories lean towards dark fiction, horror and the strange, drawing focus from the dark reality of life. His poetry is also predominantly bleak. Paul's stories have featured in several anthologies.

His debut horror novella, The Technician, is currently available to buy.

After falling in love with the work of the great Shakespeare, Morris has also drawn inspiration from Lewis Carroll, Stephen King, Graham Masterton and most notably, Michael Marshall Smith, who is still his favourite author.

In the realms of normality, Paul B Morris is happily married to an Angel, has four children who constantly get the better of him and wishes that he had the time to care for a pet bat. He owns two red t-shirts that don't suit him.

If you're interested, you can follow Paul B. Morris at www.prettytatteredsoul.com

3

TRUTH

Juan Perez

"I'm telling you the truth for the last time.
There is no such thing as a damned zombie.
That is just crap made up by Hollywood
to make money while scaring you to hell."

These were the very words I remember.
Now, with a muzzle covering your mouth
to keep you from snapping at me again,
I want to argue the point I made then.

Why don't you grunt to admit I was right?
The fact that you want to eat me proves it.
Now, I have to keep you chained up and safe.
Otherwise the living will destroy you.

Damn it, Bob! How'd you break that chain again?
Bob, listen man! I was just kidding!... Bob!

Juan Manuel Pérez is a Mexican-American poet of indigenous descent, is the current Poet Laureate for Corpus Christi, Texas (2019-2020).

4

THE LAST WALK

Matthew Cash

George's hand clasped the rail at the foot of the abbey steps as gently as he had her wrist a long time ago. His usual vitality was missing tonight but he never let that stop him before.

Almost every night he had climbed these steps. It was a ritual. It was a special place, the abbey, especially at night.

His foot lit on the step, the first step of his last ever dance. His father would bring him up here when he was young, before he was allowed to do it alone. The menfolk in his family appreciated their solitude and he followed suit.

As a teenager he would run up the hundred and ninety-nine steps, bypassing the tourists and locals egging him on, but tonight's quest was quite the struggle. He stopped to catch his breath halfway up. He hadn't stopped for at least twenty years. He ran a liver-spotted hand over his bald head; his brow speckled with sweat, "Come on old man."

That's what Lucy would've said.
George picked up his pace.

His heart beat too hard in his chest. *Too hard, too fast. Maybe I should go back?* The thought crossed his mind. "NO!" he scolded himself. He slowed but persevered.

The dark ruins of the abbey loomed in the distance, never failing to take his breath away, but this time more than normal. He doubted it was just the splendour of this mythical place.

George sat on a bench at the summit. The night was beautiful, clear, not a cloud in the sky. Millions of stars twinkled down on his seventy-three-year-old face. He reached into his coat pocket for a quick sip of whisky. His daily reward for his heroic ascent.

George made his way into the abbey grounds; he knew every contour beneath his foot like the back of her hand. The abbey walls towered above him, mighty and powerful, a world-famous landmark withstanding all weather conditions on its mighty perch upon the cliffs. How he had dreamt all his life to see it all in its original glory. A glimpse back in time to witness its construction.

Sudden, intense pain shot through George's chest, up and down his left arm. He cried out and fell against the ancient stone wall. Aftershocks of hurt surged across his chest, the epicentre his heart, and he slumped onto the grass onto his back. Through tears, he saw the night sky and the most impressive remaining piece of the abbey's structure, the Rose Window, a bright star shining through its central point.

He lay on the cool grass in agony, someone beside him touched his hand. He grimaced and started to ask them for help, but as he turned toward his saviour he was lost for words.

Death gripped his heart harder.

A girl of about seven or eight grinned down at him. Long hair ran golden down her back, kept from her face with a blue band, like a stream through a cornfield. George was startled, he remembered another girl she resembled sixty-five years ago.

His dad had a bountiful haul from his last trip at sea and had given him a little extra for his pocket. Even though George was a keen saver, he couldn't resist the rum and raisin that Old Mr Hughes made and sold in his homemade fudge shop. The fudge was so rich and creamy and melted in his mouth, it was an addiction hard to break. He had been telling Old Mr Hughes about his father catching enough fish and crabs to feed the whole of Whitby for a month. Old Mr Hughes was ever enthusiastic and laughed and nodded in all the right places.

George put his money on the counter and was putting his fudge in his school satchel when the bell on the door rang and a girl ran into the shop. He jumped at the sudden intrusion and dropped his fudge all over the floor. Cursing quietly to himself, he crouched down to retrieve it when Lucy Walker, a girl from his school who had never spoken to him before, grabbed him excitedly by the hand and yelled, "Come quickly George Fenchurch, you won't believe your eyes!"

George looked wild-eyed at Old Mr Hughes who returned his gaze with equal bewilderment and chuckled as Lucy half-dragged George away from his shop.

"Quick follow me!" Lucy cried as she pulled him along by his hand, her long blonde hair streaming behind her as they ran towards the abbey steps.

"What's going on? What's going on? This better be good, I've dropped my fudge," George complained as he tried to keep up with her as she sped up the steps like the devil was on her tail.

All she said in reply was, "Hurry up, this is better, the fudge will be there tomorrow, this won't!"

They climbed the steps as quick as they could. George noticed Lucy glance over her left shoulder in the direction of the harbour.

What's going on?

Finally, when they reached the top, George hoped she would stop, but Lucy ran past St Mary's Church and stared and pointed down over the harbour, out to sea.

George didn't need to ask what she was pointing at; it was impossible not to see.

Over the water, about two, maybe three miles out to sea, was a gigantic waterspout, a thick, white snake stretching out of the sea and into the clouds like water beneath the surface of a bath going down a plug hole, only a million times bigger. A small fishing trawler rocked perilously close. George could only imagine the terror of the people on board.

He stood beside her open-mouthed, too shocked to blink, let alone speak.

Lucy leant into him, but her eyes were still mesmerised by the colossal spout. "Isn't it magnificent?" She said and squeezed his hand.

George couldn't find the words to describe how magnificent it was; he just stared, gobsmacked at the beautiful freak of nature, and held onto the hand he would never let go of.

After a while, to their disappointment, the waterspout dispersed and vanished into nothing, first severing connection with the sea and then slowly evaporating.

It was only then George spoke, "It's a good job my dad went fishing yesterday!"

Lucy giggled at him, and for the rest of the day, they ran around St Mary's and the abbey grounds, chasing one another talking about the giant waterspout. Lucy told him all about Dracula and how the boat that brought him to England docked here in this very town. George sat and listened intently, hanging on her every word but at the back of his mind was concerned with the outcome of his rum and raisin.

George looked at the girl beside him, she was exactly the same. The pain in his chest was constantly reaching new heights, a spear through his heart, pinning him to the ground. His vision blurred and the stars above his head swirled like cream stirred into black coffee and he passed out.

He sat with Lucy Walker on a picnic blanket. The sun was glorious and the weather not too hot, but it was one of those days where you could get sunburnt without even feeling it. They had been going together since they were teenaged. He surprised her, a picnic lunch for her twenty-first birthday. She hadn't changed much from the first time he came up to the abbey thirteen years previous. She still had her pretty beautiful blonde hair and still wore a blue band to tame it.

Excitement fluttered in his belly as he watched her nibble a piece of pork pie. He filled two glasses with white wine and offered one to his girlfriend. "Well, happy twenty-first birthday Lucy," he said as they chinked glasses and drank through smiles. "I've got you a little something to commemorate our first official meeting; you can have your other present later," he said with a wink and withdrew a brown paper bag from his jacket pocket.

Lucy's eyes lit up as she took the bag and opened it, "Ha ha ha, rum and raisin fudge! It should be me buying you some. It was me who made you spill yours!" She leant forward and kissed him on the cheek.

George pulled his hand from his pocket and felt his heart beat quicker, "Give us a bit then."

Lucy offered the open bag and George delved inside and plucked a piece of the creamy brown produce and held it between his thumb and forefinger. Lucy smiled and drank her wine.

"Are you not going to have some?" George said impatiently, toying with his nugget of fudge, "Mr Hughes made it this morning."

"Oh well George, you know how I'm watching my figure, but I suppose one piece won't hurt," Lucy slid her fingers into the bag and, as if bitten by a snake, recoiled and hid her mouth with a hand. The bag fell to the grass spilling fudge pieces.

George's heart stopped. Icy invisible fingers crept down his spine.

Lucy lowered her hand and revealed the biggest smile he had ever seen. She reached back into the bag and took out the engagement ring.

Without giving him time to propose, she sprang across knocking food and wine everywhere and landed on top of him planting the hardest of kisses on his lips, "Oh god George, yes, I will marry you, yes yes yes!"

They lay together for hours making shapes out of the clouds and unbeknownst to them at the time, getting burnt red like lobsters by the afternoon sun.

George regained consciousness and tried to prop himself up on one elbow, but it was useless, the pain intolerable. He wondered where this little girl's parents were, someone that young shouldn't be out at this time of night on her own. Turning to face her he finally realised who she was.

Fifty years after they were engaged, Lucy had died.

George laid a tray of fruit, natural yoghurt, tea and toast and slipped quietly into their bedroom using his back to shield Lucy's gaze from her special birthday breakfast treat. He turned around with the opening words to happy birthday on his lips when he saw her and felt himself shatter.

Lucy, on her back, half beneath the bed sheets, her eyes glazed over, looking slightly to George's left. There was no life in them at all.

"Oh, dear God no!" was all that he could say as he placed the breakfast tray on the dresser. She would tell him off if he spilt it. He knelt and touched his hand to her cheek; it was soft but ice cold. One hand hung from beneath the duvet, George clung to it and pressed it to his face. Tears followed.

After calling for an ambulance he sat and mourned.

The pain was easing, the stars shone upon where George Fenchurch lay in the ruins of Whitby Abbey, an old man lying clutching his chest, his face ashen. "I wonder how many people have died on this land, on this very spot," he whispered feeling himself get weaker. The girl to his right squeezed his hand in reassurance. George looked at the brightest star shining through the centre of the Rose Window, his favourite piece of the abbey. As the star brightened George's pain subsided and everything other than the Rose Window grew dark, the star the light at the end of a very long tunnel. George knew it was the end.

The girl helped him to his knees and George left his earthly body. He was eight years old again now he was dead. He turned to the girl holding his hand and smiled. Lucy Walker smirked down at him and pointed up towards the bright, shining star, "Come quickly George Fenchurch, you won't believe your eyes!"

Matthew Cash, or Matty-Bob Cash as he is known to most, was born and raised in Suffolk; which is the setting for his debut novel, Pinprick. He is compiler and editor of Death by Chocolate, a chocoholic horror Anthology and the 12 Days: STOCKING FILLERS Anthology. In 2016 he launched his own publishing house, Burdizzo Books, and took shit-hot editor and author Em Dehaney on board to keep him in shape and together they brought into existence, SPARKS: an electrical horror anthology, The Reverend Burdizzo's Hymn Book, Under The Weather* and Visions From the Void **. He also has numerous solo releases on Kindle and several collections available in paperback.
Originally with Burdizzo Books, the intention was to compile charity anthologies a few times a year, but his creation has grown into something so much more powerful *insert mad laughter here*. He is currently working on numerous projects. His third novel, FUR was launched in 2018. *With Back Road Books **With Jonathan Butcher. He has always written stories since he first learnt to write and most, although not all, tend to slip into the many layered murky depths of the Horror genre.

His influences range from (when he first started reading to present day), to name but a small, select few; Roald Dahl, James Herbert, Clive Barker, Stephen King, Stephen Laws, and more. Most recently he enjoys Adam Nevill, F.R Tallis, Michael Bray, Gary Fry, William Meikle and Iain Rob Wright (who featured Matty-Bob in his famous A-Z of Horror title M is For Matty-Bob, plus Matthew wrote his own version of events which was included as a bonus).

He is a father of two, a husband of one and a zookeeper of numerous fur babies. You can find him here:

www.facebook.com/pinprickbymatthewcash

5

BUTTERFLY KISSES

Vanessa Caraveo

The second hand on the large antique wall clock
Appears to move painfully slow
And echoes throughout my grandfather's sombre bedroom
As if to announce an eternal rest is imminent.

He rests quietly with eyes closed shut
And his thin-lipped mouth slightly open
I can see his chest languidly rise up and down
His cold pale thin hand which I hold in mine
Twitches momentarily
I squeeze his hand slightly tighter.

For it feels as only yesteryear
He held me in his arms as a little girl
And helped me blow out my birthday cake candles
When I turned six.

How proud he was to see my school report card
When I achieved high grades each semester
And he would boast to his mature friends

THE LAST TIME

Of what a bright and wonderful granddaughter he had.
After my birth
Mother and I faced hardships
We moved in with my grandfather at his humble home
Which he was generous to offer
His unconditional love and support
        Knew no boundaries.

A few days ago, while he was briefly conscious
He looked over to where I sat at his bedside
Reached over to embrace my hand
And told me with an unforgettable smile
How much I meant to him
And how he always
        saw me as a daughter.

Remembering this I shed a tear
Knowing this was the last time I would hear his voice
I lean over and my quivering lips touch his cool forehead
I softly plant him butterfly kisses
And whisper in his ear
        You will always be my father.

Vanessa Caraveo is an award-winning author and published poet who has been avidly involved in writing throughout the years. She is a writer for various non-profit groups and organizations and works closely with them to promote inclusion for all. Her poetry has been published in various anthologies and organisations in which she hopes to uplift the lives of others through her literary work through this noble craft.

6

EVE'S EXIT INTERVIEW

Matt McGee

"Here's what you don't know," Eve said.

She sat up proper in her chair, back rigid and legs crossed as a woman of refinement and experience prefers to do. She leaned toward the interviewers phone, set on the desk between them.

"Is this thing on?"

"It's rolling," the interviewer said.

"Rolling? That's a pretty old term for someone so young."

"Call it what you like. It's going."

"I can't tell. It's taken me a while to get used to technology. I mean, here you guys are, all these thousands of years later having dug up Adam and I, replicated our DNA and brought us back to life. So, you could do what? Hear what really happened that day at the apple tree?"

"That's exactly what the public is dying to know."

"Well, they've certainly waited long enough."

"And you've been somewhat of a mystery ever since. First hiding out in the JPL lab. Then the big house in Pacific Palisades. You've been hard to reach since being brought back."

"Can you imagine going thousands of years into the future and trying to adjust?"

"I can imagine. So, can we go over the story of the garden?"

"Again with the garden. Fine. This is the last time."

"You were about to talk," the interviewer redirected, "about something we didn't know."

"You hear all about what happened that day at the apple tree. Me, the serpent, blah blah blah. But here's what you don't know."

The interviewer waited.

"There were fifty-one of us." Eve leaned back, as if allowing that to sink in.

"I'm sorry. Did you say -"

"Yeah, fifty-one. Me, Adam, and forty-nine bimbos running around without anything on but last fall's offerings. He had fifty of us to choose from. Not just me. Adam had his pick of the litter. Go figure. And good Lord I was sick of it."

The interviewer nodded gently. "These other women. What were their names?"

"Oh wow, it's been so long. Let's see. There was Tiffany. Krista – she was a blonde. Allison, Laura, Caitlin, who else? The one who invented fire, what was her name? Beth or something like that."

The interviewer waited. "These other forty-nine women. What happened to them?"

"Good question. And since I think the statute of limitations ran out quite some time ago, I'm going to give you the juiciest story you've ever had."

The interviewer waited.

"I killed them."

The interviewer looked unimpressed. "If this is true, why did archaeologists find only two sets of remains? You and Adam? Where are the remains of these other forty-nine?"

"Ascended, I suppose."

The interviewer grew a look now, one of pure scepticism that borders on pity for a pathological liar.

"Ascended to where?"

"Heaven. After they ate the apples."

"Which apples?"

Eve rolled her eyes. "You act like you don't know this part of the story or something."

The interviewer looked at Eve, deadpan. "The Old and New testaments left out the part about Eve killing off her competition."

"That's exactly what happened! And I'm here to set the record straight." Eve arched her back as if a moment of triumph had happened.

"OK," the interviewer smiled, "supposing for a moment that you bumped off Tiffany, and Krista, and…."

"Beth…"

"Right. Beth the Firestarter. Supposing you off'ed all these other girls. *Why* did you do it?"

"You act like you've never seen a beauty pageant."

"Actually, I'm surprised *you* have."

Eve looked away a moment. She seemed to be searching for something. She stood up, crossed the room to her purse, pulled out a pack of cigarettes and lit one.

"Those aren't good for you."

Eve scoffed. "You're just going to regenerate my DNA all over again, right?" She took a long drag and blew it toward the ceiling.

"These other forty-nine. You said they 'ascended.' Did they float off into the sky or something?"

"Well not exactly. We had tigers."

"Tigers."

"Yes."

"As pets?"

"*No.* Duh. Outside the garden. They weren't allowed into our compound. Once I'd bumped off one of the others I'd wait until nightfall then heave their body up over the wall. I'd have to assume the tigers took them."

"This is all very enlightening."

"I did it for a reason."

"I'm sure you did."

"You ever date a guy who wouldn't commit?"

"Hmm. More than once."

"Well imagine the guy, the *only* guy at that, had fifty options."

"He'd be pretty hard to nail down."

"You bet your sweet Pilate'd butt he would. If humanity was going to survive, we were going to have to thin out the herd a little."

"Down to just you."

Eve hit the cigarette again. She nodded. "Eventually, yes."

"Wouldn't humanity have had a better chance if Adam were consummating his existence with all fifty of you?"

"Not the point."

"Sure. Safety in numbers."

Eve shrugged. "Maybe. Who cares? We're not talking about them. Wasn't this supposed to be about me? How I got to be the first, the Earth Mother."

"How did you decide who you were going to get rid of?"

"Good question. Usually it was on bathing day. Whoever looked the most fit, the prettiest, whoever seemed to have the most talent, that's who I'd bump off. Couldn't have that kind of competition."

The interviewer nodded. "Funny you put it like that."

Eve hit her cigarette once more and ground it out. "Like what?"

"Well you say there were fifty of you."

"Yes."

"Like there are fifty states."

Eve kept mute. She eyed her cigarette pack.

"And you 'eliminated your competition,' usually while…"

"In our bathing suits, yes."

"Right. What was the name of the last one you bumped off?"

"That I remember. Nina. Nina was her name."

"Nina Davuluri?"

Eve waved a hand. "I didn't have time to get last names. I knocked her out and over the wall she went."

"Dark skinned? Bright eyes? Arched eyebrows?"

"Sounds like her. Why are you asking so many questions about this woman? She doesn't matter. What matters is me. I made it. I'm the winner."

"Actually, Nina was the winner."

Eve looked at the interviewer.

"Nina Davuluri is the current Miss America. Did you watch it on television?"

Eve sat quietly a moment. She crossed her arms over her chest.

"Perhaps Eve," the interviewer said quietly, "you're making up a bit of history since you don't actually have any to remember."

Eve said nothing.

The interviewer clicked her phone and a new file began recording. "Now, let's start over. In the beginning," she said.

"In the beginning," Eve said, "there was just me. And Adam."

The interviewer waited.

"And two other women, Rachel and Phoebe. We lived in this tall house up in a tree, and there were two other men, Joey and Chandler -"

The interviewer clicked the phone off again. "Stop it! What have you been doing since the scientists brought you back?"

Eve said nothing. The two sat in silence a long while. Finally, the interviewer took a long look Eve's way.

"Is that all you've done since being brought back to life, watched TV?"

Eve stayed silent. She nodded.

The interviewer put her phone away.

"Does it matter?" Eve burst out. "I mean, what do we remember of history nowadays that isn't either done on The History Channel or looked up on Wikipedia? TV *is* our history!"

The interviewer slung her bag over her shoulder and stood to leave. "No," she said, "it isn't. But *you* are. And it would be nice if you could remember some of it to enlighten us."

Eve slumped in her chair. "Yes. It would be nice. But... I'm sorry."

The interviewer looked down at her with pity.

"I'm sorry," Eve repeated. "I don't remember being there. For the last time, I don't remember anything."

The interviewer reached in her bag. She took out a business card and slipped it on the desk in front of Eve.

"If you do remember something, call or email me."

Eve said nothing. She nodded. The interviewer walked to the front door of the hillside home and closed it behind her.

Eve heard the car leave the driveway. She looked down at the card, silent, perfectly still.

After a few moments she stood, crossed to a couch, picked up the remote and clicked on her flat screen. Outside the living room window the sun slipped down and ended another day in brilliant orange while inside, the room glowed with blue televised light. *Happy Days* was on. The Fonz was revving his bike, getting ready to jump his motorcycle over fourteen garbage cans.

Eve nodded and smiled. She leaned forward, elbows on knees, soaking in the images, the pensive looks on Mr. and Mrs. C's faces. As Fonzie sped up his bike toward the ramp, she cupped her hands together and thought to herself:

I remember this one. I just can't remember the last time I saw it.

Matt McGee writes short fiction in the Los Angeles area. In 2019, his stories have appeared in Poetic Diversity, Gnashing Teeth, Octillo, Biograph and 'The Rebirthing Shed' currently appears in Zimbell House's "1929" anthology. When not typing he drives around in a vintage Mazda and plays goalie in local hockey leagues.

7

THE STRUGGLE

Leanne Cooper

Numb to the point of not feeling
Heart heavy in my chest
Rapidly beating
Hands shaking so much
That I can barely hold on
To the blade between my fingers
And after I was done
I swore that it would be the last time.

Days, weeks, months
All blur into one
Time passes so quickly
the negative thoughts come creeping
voice in my head whispering
Pointing out every mistake
Everything that I say or do is wrong
Until again I fall to the blade
And I swear that it will be the last time.

Promises never last
Good mental health is not a thing I can grasp

THE LAST TIME

And despite all my healing
I can't shake this feeling
I sink deeper into a hole I cannot escape
Wishing that life would just give me a break
Then once again, I succumb
And I swear that this will be the last time.

I know that I need help
Continuously calling out
But the screams get caught in my throat
Struggling to breathe so I choke
No one understands how I'm feeling
This disease leaves me reeling
I'm trying so hard to keep afloat
But I swore before would be the last time.

Now when I'm trapped in my own head
Sinking in the depths
Unable to tread water
Not knowing where to turn or who to trust
I write it all out
Pen replaces blade, ink replaces blood
I'm learning to handle it better
Making sure that last time
will always be the last time.

Leanne Cooper is a poet and writer from the West Midlands, who has performed across the West Midlands, and Stafford. Leanne's first poetry collection, 'Awake at 3 AM' was released in March 2018, and her second collection, 'All for You' will be available soon.

8

THE LAST TIME

Nirmal Kaur Orjally

A precious life inside my womb,
Illuminated many hearts and souls
Spontaneous love grows intense,
as I carry our bundle of joy
And yet unknown, it was temporary for the last time!

I did not get to dress you in
Natural, lemon, or mint coloured outfits,
I did not get to see you smile,
touch your newborn skin, or watch you blow raspberries
I did not get to tickle your toes, cradle you, or love you for
the last time!

Emptiness, loss, and grief builds higher than the Empire
State,
as l leave the hospital in lightness.
At least you are young…at least you can conceive…
At least the baby wasn't full term,
said the doctors, midwives, nurses for the last time!

Not long after, l arrived home.

Shortly, l was alone. l longed for a strong warm hug,
Wrapped tightly around me
and to hear whispers that everything
is going to be okay, for the last time!

I was determined to shift and heal from this grieving
process
I looked up at the portraits of
Sri Guru Nanak Dev ji, Sri Guru Gobind Singh Ji,
and then at the Universe. I asked for forgiveness.
A threatened miscarriage for the last time!

Nirmal was born in Hertfordshire and now lives in Wolverhampton. She work at a local school and also at Wolverhampton Wanderers Football Club. She is an active member of Blakenhall Writers Group as well as a member of Punjabi Women's Writing Group. She has performed her work on stage at Wolverhampton Central Library, City Voices, Literature Festival, Ironbridge and The Big City Radio. She has also written a children's novel, Tambi, which is as yet unpublished. She enjoys writing as it gives me a voice and allows her to express her creativity.

9

WINGMAN

Dan McKeithan

A good wingman never lets you down. And I'd had the best. We were like brothers even though we were polar opposites. I knew after we parted ways tonight, I'd never see him again. One of us wasn't coming back from this one. I should've listened to him in the first place. He'd always insisted that monsters were real.

We'd grown up next door to each other and first met when he was signalling me from his window with a flashlight on a stormy night. Of course, it would turn out that I was way off base.

He was using the light to read under the covers in his bedroom. Some horror book about vampires, werewolves, and zombies. When I flashed my light back at him, it scared him so bad he wet himself. He said they were real, but it's all fiction, right?

From that point on we were inseparable. We made an odd pair. Chet was about fifty pounds overweight with large dark glasses. I was lean and strong. The star running back for our school team. Chet couldn't get a position as water boy. He knew he was better off by hanging with me.

He was always by my side and always had my back. Not long after high school our relationship took a different turn. We'd scope out every bar in town and beyond. He'd find the women and bring them to me. Never once did he want one for himself—not until this past week.

It all started out at a small country western bar that we spotted on the side of the road on the outskirts of town. It had to have been an old biker hang out because there was no way it would have been able to stay open this far out without a steady group coming and going. But the night we found it, there were only a couple of bikes out front. Chet pointed it out and we pulled into the gravel lot.

The outside looked as if dirt was all that kept it from falling. The inside was a different story. It sparkled with a vibrant life. The bartender, a muscled man in an old t-shirt was wiping the bar. There were only a handful of customers. The tables were set in a pattern so all the patrons could watch the real action from a stage in the front.

The most alluring woman I'd ever seen was singing. I knew then that I had to meet her. Chet brought us over a couple of long necked beers, and I pointed her out to him.

"What do you see in her?" He asked. "She's at least twice your age."

"How can you not see it," I said. "Check her out; she can't be that much older than us. And that voice."

"I guess age is relative, man, but…"

I slammed my fist down on the table. My vision blurred slightly as the beer began to take effect awful fast. The table shook with dust and wobbled. I blinked and everything was fine. The place was clean and well kept. My head was out of sorts. "She's the one for tonight."

"What about Brandy, from the other night?" Chet asked. "You said she was awesome, and I thought maybe you guys hit it off."

"I hit it alright, but no sparks."

Chet had never fought me before. I'd always thought maybe he was into me and not women. He never dated or tried to ask a girl out. He was more interested in his horror books and his obsession with monsters. I should have realized then that something was off, but I just chalked it up to him trying to grow a backbone.

After another round he walked over to the stage and began chatting with the singer. I watched him hand her a piece of paper. My phone number?

I'd never felt so nervous before. Just the anticipation of him waving me over and introducing me to her was making me break out into a sweat. I hoped my odour wouldn't drive her off. Could this be what real feelings were like? I'd never made a commitment with a woman before or ever had to worry what they thought of me, but this was different.

Chet came back to our table with a glum look. "No luck, dude," he said. "She's got a boyfriend and isn't on the market."

I was so mad; I saw stars. My eyes teared up and for one moment the bar swam with dust and debris, then my vision cleared with my head. "Screw her. I'll go and tell her what she's missing." I stood to go, and Chet grabbed me by my arm.

"Let this one go, Rick," he said. "She's not in your league. Let's get outta here." With that he threw some cash on the bar and dragged me from the room.

Outside in the moonlight he took me by my shirt collar. "Have you ever stared into the eyes of the devil and not blinked?"

I pushed him off of me. "What the hell?"

He was so excited his whole face was dripping with sweat. "I've always told you they were real, but you wouldn't listen..."

"Seriously, you have a screw loose," I said. "Come on, let's go home."

He finally agreed and we drove back to town in silence. I couldn't wait for him to leave. I was going back. Nothing was keeping me from her.

I dropped him off at his Volvo and waited a few moments for him to drive away. Once he was gone, I high tailed it to the bar.

Imagine my surprise when I noticed his Volvo was already in the lot. I slammed on my breaks and rushed inside. He was nowhere in sight, but she was.

She stood by the bar finishing up a glass of something that looked like scotch. I walked over to her and stuck out my hand. "Rick Lowman, I'm sure you noticed me from earlier."

She paused and looked me over as if trying to place me. Then she hesitantly laid her hand in mine. "Sheila, but we've never met."

"I won the all state finals two years ago. I'm sure you've heard of me. I was in here tonight with the other guy, kinda awkward and big. He came over and talked to you about me..."

She shook her head.

"He's got to be here. His car's out front."

Her eyes lit up. "Big beefy hunk?" she asked. "He left with Jack, the bartender."

She must've seen the confusion in my eyes. She smiled and took me by the arm. "Come with me," she said. "My place is next door. Your friend and Jack are at my house."

I begrudgingly let her lead me out the back door to a small house. Maybe this could still turn out okay.

"Don't mind my mom," Shelia said. "She's usually in the living room, knitting. But she doesn't speak."

"No problem," I said. I was hoping to spend as little time socializing as possible.

She led me to the porch and opened the door. The living room lamp was on and a sweet looking older lady sat rocking in a chair, knitting. I started to sit down on the couch.

She jerked me up. And for a brief second my vision swam. The room appeared greyed out. The little old woman was a rotted corpse, her jaw hanging from her head. The floor was littered with bones and bodies. Chet's body lay on the couch. His eyes were dead; blood ran from holes in his neck.

An aged corpse wearing the muscle shirt of the bartender lay on the floor with a stake sticking out of it.

I stared at Shelia. She appeared yellowed with age and wrinkled with bits of her hair having fallen out in clumps. Her eyes, dark and red, bore into mine. How could you not blink?

Then the room was normal. Shelia's arm was around me; bringing me in for a kiss.

"I'm looking for a new bartender. How are you on mixed drinks?" She asked.

And now I'm her wingman.

Dan McKeithan completed his MFA in Creative Fiction from UC-Riverside in 2016 while fighting off cancer. Prior to that he attended UCLA in Professional Screenwriting in 2002 while working for Warner Bros Studios as security for the TV show EXTRA. Now his day job is running two nursing homes in North Carolina and when he's not at home or off in Russia with his wife's family he tries to get a little writing done. He is also a member of the Horror Writers Association and enjoys reading most any type of horror stories.

10

LAST TIME IT LOOKED DIFFERENT

Norbert Góra

The last time I died
I remembered it all differently,
there was no corridor,
all I saw was a tunnel,
now, for a change,
empty walls greet me,
their whiteness repels
like a picture of violence,
step by step towards the curtain
woven from fog (the seamstress has talent),
another check-in and I'm ready,
death will pass me into
the arms of life again.

Norbert Góra is a 29 years old poet and writer from Poland. He is the author of more than 100 poems which have been published in poetry anthologies in USA, UK, India, Nigeria, Kenya and Australia.

THE LAST TIME

11

LOVE IS AN ALPHABET

Jan Hedger

Awakening to the sun's weak rays; only just managing to filter through the voile curtain, draped gypsy style, covering the expanse of cheap double glazing; Leah let the music wash over her. *Blue Moon, you saw me standing alone...*

Choking back the lump forming in her dry throat, Leah scolded herself; it's only a song, with words written by someone who didn't even know her. Didn't know how longingly, she had, as a young girl, stared through a single pane of glass, as the cycle of the moon, rotated with the passing into womanhood.

Echoing the dulcet tone, *without a dream in my heart,* Leah stayed one beat behind, her cognitive skills a little slower now. Feeling for the volume switch, she allowed the song to rise, to lift her back, to the night she saw him across the dance floor. Gracefully the couples had swept between them and she had longed to join in, to feel the freedom of lifting feet, in pulsating abeyance to the singer, crooning his tune in time with the band, *you knew just what I was there for.* Heady from the two glasses of Champagne, she had found herself smiling openly at him, as he returned her gaze through the moving bodies.

Ill at ease with the fabric of her frock, not falling below her knees, Leah recalled trying to pull it down against all its stiffened resistance. Just like her mother, the material hadn't given an inch.

Keeping her wandering mind focused was challenging, but she must get to the end of the song, or else she may have lost him forever.

Leah once more let the only remaining clear memories engulf her frail mind.

'May I have the pleasure of asking you to dance?' Nervously, his tremulous voice had caused her to lift her eyes from the fixation of seeing her shapely calves encased only in sheer nylon.

Oh, the temerity of saying, 'yes, of course you may' caused her heart to leap, even now – as the song continued, *and then there suddenly appeared before me, the only one my arms will ever hold.*

Putting her slim hand into his, she had allowed him to lead her directly under the mirrored glitter ball, its twinkling light illuminating dancing patches of fairy dust on the polished floor. Quivering at first, like two birds in new flight, they had let the music lead them, melting into the 4/4 time of the Foxtrot. Rotating together, two as one combined, eyes locked, her blue moon had turned to gold.

She remembered getting home late, her mother waiting, the hand across the face, and not even in her grave (which would come soon enough) would she ever forget. Tears threatened to break, and Leah automatically stroked her cheek still feeling the sharp sting of pain that shattered her beautiful evening.

Uselessly she had pleaded, and locked in her room, the only moonlight came through the unchanging pane of glass. Vacant years followed, till her mother breathed her last, releasing her, but it was too late.

Without a dream in my heart – without a love of my own, Leah's broken voice cried at the radio, "but I had a love once, real love - Xavier, I want to dance, are you there?"

THE LAST TIME

Yellow sunlight, a mellow shade of gold fell upon the coverlet, embracing Leah's cold face. Zephyr wind, warm from the west, carried his answer and putting her wrinkled hand into his, she allowed him to lead her directly under the rotating glitter ball.

Jan Hedger started writing in 2001 in her hometown of Birmingham; after living away in Berkshire, Wiltshire, Sussex and North East Scotland; and now lives in Chirk, North Wales.
She has had poetry published in anthologies and regularly performs her work at Open Mic events, and with 'Puppets, Poetry and Reminiscence'. With her husband she is one half of 'Poet and the Piano Player'.
Jan has self-published two poetry books, and in 2013 produced 'Our Friends & Their Habitats' – Near & Far, a Pot Pourri of animal poems.
In 2018 she took part in organising, and running events for The Wilfred Owen Festival in Oswestry .
Jan leads her own writing group; Words'n'pics Open Writers known as WOW.

12

ONLY ONE

Leon Roy

Free electricity of the Atmosphere
Baby Blue positively charged
My negativity grounds me
Like the sole of my boot
Surface tension broken
My relief wrapped in plastic
The only promise
Etched as a warning
Anchored by a chemical vapor
Immoral *American Spirits*

Burning fossil fuels from my
Wrinkled stick of white
Toxic gas like Carbon Monoxide
A well-formed Cumulus Cloud
Following me like a nightmare
The impending storm lingers
Never dissipates
Only here to remind me of
My Somber
My year packed tightly within my palm

A Supernova between my fingers
Creeping toward the ash of my skin
With its Cancerous glow
The slow-burning ember
Yellow-orange
Caught in expanding emptiness
I flick it away and escape to Evergreen
Jaywalking through a Cemetery of
White Dwarfs
They lay dormant above Tar and Granite

Motherless clouds mock me
Breathing as I choke
Thunder and Lightning strike
My shallow chest, rapid
Lungs shriveling like spinach in
A piping hot pan
Killing me softly
Metamorphosed
I'm a sickly yellow
Raw with bitter withdrawal

Inhale, exhale
My blood pressure boils off
Like a Phoenix born of
Angela's Ashes
Protection a worthless recessed filter
The smoldering ember *Parliament*
My nerves digging deep with the worms
Breaching the soil to crawl
Night crawlers crawl and crawl and crawl
Starving the Marina

The Supermassive black hole takes me back
Stretching me thin
My flickering flame no match
For its gravitational pull

THE LAST TIME

Colour me luminous blue
A Supernova Imposter
The black between Heavens light
The Sun and Paper Moons
Ecstasy strengthens my weakness
Intoxicated and bound

Cast away by Society to
Designated smoky corners
I retreat to my Garden of Wallflowers
Where the roots intertwine and weave
The flame burning twice as bright
But half as long
Like a Hypergiant
Alienated and Alone
Remembering only one became twenty
Then twenty more. Twenty more

I'm blemished and bruised
Like rotting fruit
Catching my flies with Honey and Vinegar
Crushed underneath black/grey soot
Like the straw that broke the
Camel's back
I'll be buried six feet deep
With the Night crawlers
Just one last, last pack for my year
The White Dwarfs my company

Leon Roy is a poet, writer, and author of the new poem *"Only One."* Leon's focus in recent years has transitioned from screenplays to dark fiction Novels and Novellas that showcase his poetry. His life-long love of film and classic literature creates a unique voice that shines through his writing style. His first short story, *"A Lovely Little Nash,"* was also his first publication, set in the horror anthology *"Northern Frights."* Leon is a family man, dedicating time between his wife and three kids to display an artistic view on varying genres. A Maine native, Leon can be found playing piano during his downtime or reading his favourite poet, *Sylvia Plath*. Leon can be contacted via private email at tquirion1992@gmail.com.

THE LAST TIME

13

LOVE AT LAST SIGHT

James Josiah

I remember the first time I saw her, all pink lipstick smirk and a flash of mischief in those beautiful pale blue grey eyes. It wasn't love at first sight or anything as cliché as that. If anything, that would have been preferable. It would have been so much easier to deal with that than what happened to us in the end.

We had both found ourselves at the same bar to see the same band play their first headline gig. We had both convinced ourselves they were going to be the next big thing and were there to be able to say that we had seen Chekhov's Gun play the Rose and Crown on a dreary October night. Evidently a lot of people had the same idea as the place was rammed. There was a buzz in the air, one that I hadn't felt since I saw Fungus open for Terrorvision back in 2005.

I will admit that I easily get over excited about new bands and have declared many of my discoveries to be the next big thing, but the way I look at it you only have to get it right once don't you? And I have come very close at times, I imported Limp Bizkit's debut album and told anyone who listened they were going to be huge and they were. You can argue amongst yourselves about the quality of their output but none of you can deny that they were massive. Yeah, for every My Chemical Romance there are a dozen Leaf Eaters or Llama Farmers, but at the time I honestly thought they were the best thing I had ever seen.

That's pretty much how I felt the first time I saw her. Like I say, the place was absolutely packed, but she was clearly the coolest person in the room. She was there on her own, stood at the back, bottle of lager in one hand steadily drumming the beat out against the neck using one the many rings that graced her fingers. I was there on my own as well and I was very aware of the fact I had ordered just the one pint then gone on to stand to the side of the stage with all the other sad cases. She just had this sort of aura, this vibe, this air of just not caring what anyone thought. She was on her own because she had chosen to be, not because everyone was tired of her rabbiting on about yet another two-bit band.

I never spoke to her that night. I was too in awe of her and knew I would only end up saying something stupid and I didn't want to come across like an absolute tool from the off. That has happened too many times in the past and I knew then I wanted to get to know her properly. I needed to.

Before we get too far into this, I want to make it clear that I'm not a stalker, or some type of pervy peeping Tom. I never followed her anywhere. I didn't find out where she lived or worked. All I did was try to be places that I thought she might also be at.

It sounds bad when I say it out loud like that, but it wasn't creepy, or at least it wasn't meant to be. I'm quite an awkward fella. Very aware of my faults and deathly afraid of them. I know I'm not a looker and have the animal magnetism of a haddock, so if I was going to get to know her it would have to be as friends, and she was so cool that I was sure it would be enough.

I got it wrong a lot of times. She never went to any of the open mic nights dotted around town. I never found out what pub she considered to be her local. She would just appear, seemingly at random, at gigs. Always on her own. Always with that same almost detached air of ice-cold coolness.

We first spoke at the Black Asteroids EP launch; I'd been into them since the weirdly disastrous gig at the old Rainbow. They were opening for Lionize, a band I first saw supporting Clutch. I first saw Clutch when they opened for Corrosion of Conformity, but that's a story for another day. The main point here is Black Asteroids were a support band for a support band of a support band. Lionize had just released their new album and had come over from the States to promote it. Everything pointed at a band very much on the rise so there was no way I was going to miss it.

There were seven people there, including me. Everyone involved was frankly baffled and various things were blamed - from the booking agent, to a lack of promo by the venue, to social media algorithms. Whatever it was that kept people away was criminal as both bands played their socks off that night.

I'm not sure why she was at the EP launch as I had seen Black Asteroids every single time they had played locally since the Rainbow incident and had never seen her at any of them. I was so shocked to see her that I ended up speaking to her accidently. I was stood at the merch stand talking to Duncan the sound engineer, asking him how you even go about micing up a xylophone never mind two of them, and she just sort of appeared from nowhere, leant in and said *"Not that it really matters but they are actually glockenspiels."*

All I managed to say in return was *"Oh."*

That was it. *"Oh"*. All those months of traipsing around town, trying to look cool and interesting. Trying to just cross her path and make the right impression and the first thing I said to her wasn't even really a word.

"See, your glockenspiel has metal bars, whereas a xylophone's bars are wooden. They look pretty much the same I guess but the sounds are massively different…"

She stopped talking suddenly, I still can't decide if it's because she had run out of glockenspiel trivia or if she heard what she was saying and decided to stop before it got worse. I mean where do you go from there? The Marimba? The Vibraphone? She was starting to blush and the mischief in her eyes was slowly being swallowed by panic.

It felt like forever, but really could have been only a few seconds, and I was very aware that I was not only staring but also not saying anything. In the end I managed to utter *"Hi, I'm Dean."* I even offered her a hand to shake, which is polite but maybe a little overly formal for a scummy rock club.

Thankfully she shook my hand and said, *"Hi Dean, I'm Rose, but please don't ever call me Rosie as I hated that show when I was a kid."*

The thing about people telling you not to do things is you always immediately want to do them. My head was full of images of narrowboats, wooden ducks and a kind old man steering the way to odd little adventures. But at the end of the day I am a gentleman so didn't say her name again at all just in case it slipped out.

We spoke for a while that night; she was there as she had heard good things about the band and wanted to check them out for herself. I told her she should check out their other stuff and told her about my blog where I reviewed gigs, albums and films. She said she would but not in the way that people normally do. She said she would in a way that I might actually see a rise in traffic for once. She made her excuses, went to the bar, got herself a bottle of lager, that I immediately regretted not offering to buy, and stood at the back of the room to watch the gig. I wasn't brave enough to follow her so stood by the side of the stage with my pint and a stupid smile on my face.

The next time I saw her, she approached me. We were at another Chekhov's Gun gig even though by this time it was obvious that they weren't the next big thing after all. The mischief in her eyes had been replaced by a fire and her cool air was now an electric buzz of excitement. She told me she had read my blog.

No one ever reads my blog. I have to force myself to stop looking at the traffic stats as it depresses me and makes me feel like I am wasting my time, but she had read it. She had read all of it, trawling backwards through years of my rambling about music and cinema. Through my dreadful attempts at prose and poetry and that one post where I pitched a soap opera where the cast were all animal puppets. She had read it all and still wanted to talk to me! She had read it and then come to find me to talk about it all.

She said she had an idea. If we're being honest, I was onboard from the off, but I let her try and convince me as watching her jump back and forward across the details was enthralling. She was a web developer by day and a photographer on the side. She said how if we worked together we could build... something. She wasn't quite sure if it was a website or maybe a fanzine, if we wanted to go retro, but she knew that my words and her pictures belonged together. Belonged together, those were the words she actually used.

We ducked out of the gig before Chekhov's Gun had even played a note. We needed somewhere quiet to flesh out her idea. Somewhere to talk over the fine points. Would we pigeonhole ourselves to one genre or cover the full spectrum of stuff out there? Should we focus on the burgeoning local scene or venture further afield? Between us we figured out we already knew a lot of the big hitters of the local scene so to start we'd focus on them. And then when we got big (not if, when!), we'd use the momentum we'd built to go for bigger and bigger bands.

It felt like my brain was on fire. The blog started off as a bit of fun with dreams of maybe someone noticing what I was doing, but of late it's more of a habit and a chore than anything else. A lot of effort for no return at all. Even the spammers had stopped replying to the posts these days, but this felt new and fresh and tangible. For the first time in a long time I wanted to actually achieve something. She had given me a sense of worth that I had forgotten ever losing.

It was getting late, the barman had long called time and told us in no uncertain terms that we either left now or get locked in for the night. I offered to and then insisted on walking her to the station and while there were moments of silence, none of them were awkward. We swapped numbers saying we would catch up again soon. I'm not going to lie I wanted to kiss her right then and there, but at the end of the day I'm a coward.

I stood on the platform and watched her take a seat. The mischief was back in those beautiful, pale blue-grey eyes as she waved and smiled that pink lip-sticked smirk. As the train pulled away, she blew a pantomime kiss to me. That was the last time I ever saw her. That was when I knew that I loved her.

James Josiah is an author, editor, poet and curator of the Lost Haiku project. He has a lot of brilliant ideas and occasionally manages to pull one off. He's also one half of the dynamic duo that is Black Dream.

14

THE DIFFERENCE COUNTS THE LAST TIME

Juleigh Howard-Hobson

"What would you do?"
The question floats across the dark bedroom.
From one twin bed to another on its web of nightly repetition.

"When?"
The response is another question.
 It always is.
That's how it's supposed to be.
A build up has to occur, a structure made solid with words repeated.
Like a prayer.
But I didn't understand that yet.

"If you were here all alone…and your phone is dead."
"Where?"
"Out in the meadow, coming back through the apple trees."
"I'd run inside and grab the shotgun."

"What if there were no bullets?"
"I'd get the dogs, let them loose, then run to the Holmes farm. They have landlines."
"What if it wasn't just a person standing there, watching you, but a witch?"
"I'd run under the white oak trees."
"What if they were between you and the oak trees?"
"There's an Ash tree out there, I could get under it."
"What if it wasn't a witch, but a ghost?"
"I'd pick up an Alder twig and protect myself."
"What if the wind blew all the twigs away?"
"I'd spit in my hands, bless them and wipe it on my forehead."
"Ew, you wouldn't."
"Yes, that's how you protect yourself if you have no other way. What would you do?"
"I'd run into the forest and get the fairies to protect me."
"They don't do that."
"How do you know? They might."

Another voice interrupts, loudly. It always interrupts.
"Go to sleep!"
And we settle down. It's an old game.
Played by children brought up in the rural backwaters
Who know how lonely it gets.
We refine our strategies every night, until we are told to go to sleep.

The question lingers, remains to be revised again tomorrow.
Always. Always.
What if you see a strange figure, watching you, when you are alone out here?
We have tackled it so many times, so many ways, it isn't scary anymore.
We drift to sleep, knowing we have covered all the bases.
We'll always know exactly what to do.

Comforting in the unquestionability of it.

Until the time I am alone, and a tall dark figure appears at
the edge of the far meadow.
Watching me.
That last time I figure out the difference between knowing
what to do
and what really happens.

Juleigh Howard-Hobson's writing has appeared in many places, on and offline, including: *Coffin Bell, Noir Nation, Alien Buddha's House of Horrors, Shooter, Breach, The Ghost City Review, Non Binary Review, Abridged Magazine, The Ginger Collect, Siren's Call, HipMama, Here Comes Everyone, Panopoly, Postcard Poems and Prose, Autumn Sky, Anima, Riddled with Arrows,* "The Literary Whip" (the podcast of the Nonbinary Review), I Am Strength (Blind Faith Books), The Nancy Drew Anthology (Silver Birch), Mandragora (Scarlett Imprint), Glory of Man: The Rise and Fall of the Reality Soldier (Cockroach Conservatory), Under The Light of A Neon Moon (Madville Publishing), The 2018 Rhysling Anthology (The Science Fiction Poetry Association) and many other venues.

She edited an Arêtes Vakreste Boker award winning Norwegian anthology: Undertow and served as assistant poetry editor at *Able Muse*. She's a Million Writers Award "Notable Story" writer and her work has earned an Alfred Award, an Anzac Award, as well as being a Predators and Editor's top ten finisher. She has been nominated for the Best of the Net, the Pushcart Prize and the Rhysling, and recently has had a poem honoured with an Orison Anthology nomination.

She currently has five books published to her name, the most recent being a collection called Our Otherworld (The Red Salon Press, 2018).

15

MISSING

Samantha Dewally

I should stop watching.
Switch off, swipe right.
But it has become a silent obsession –
a learned helplessness creating this passive, fatalistic
spectator.
A synaptic pruning has disturbed vital routes to reasoned
thought -
Fizzing hormones rewiring the old grey matter.

Despair has scraped its burrow where once resided my
Anger.
With curled, clawed fists it floats, gleeful.
Thus silenced, the images scream from backlit screens and
settle into the cradle of my arms.
I stroke their pallid cheeks as undigested morsels splatter
my senses.
And in those darkest hours I feast,
delicious salty lips scoop each splendid drop into the cold,
rusting ash-pan of my belly.

Like my child, my Anger has

moved
on.

My child said goodbye at least, skipping carelessly into
adulthood,
But my anger left when I wasn't looking.
She dripped silently into maternity pads
Whilst softened eyes were directed downwards at new life.
I was too busy, you see, cooing gentle songs,
to notice her seeping through my clothes and evaporate…

I picture my anger on the News, an appeal for the Missing.
Behind closed lids, I observe her decaying in a roadside
ditch with wide, dull eyes staring.
The last time I saw her she was leaning on the doorframe,
arms folded.
That stance of defiance, as with raised chin she flounced
downstairs,
rucksack of righteous indignation rattling the banister rails.
I miss her, you see, as I observe this world.

Samantha Dewally likes to paddle in lots of artistic puddles: acapella singing,
mixed media art and poetry. A linguist by training, she lived abroad for many
years and has since worked in education and community arts. Sam has recently
relocated to the foothills of Cader Idris in South Snowdonia. It is said that those
who sleep on the slopes of the mountain will awaken either as a madman or a
poet. Sam remains hopeful.

16

LAST TIME

Richard Archer

Do you remember our last time?
Afterwards you said loving me had turned into a hate
crime,
as I'd changed so little, while you'd grown so much,
I tried to hold you but you recoiled from my touch.
Then when you'd left as I lay there wishing I was dead,
the clever words came to me I wished that I'd said.

I'll never forget our last time,
as I tried to capture it all in words and rhyme.
Imagining that if I put my memories on the page
we'd be together forever until the end of days.
However because of the way my fractured reflection goes,
which of us was right or wrong no one will ever know.

Richard Archer is a well-known, much loved poet from Walsall. He's the
Chairman of Walsall Poetry Society, a writer of too many books and one part of
FreeVerse Walsall's spoken word festival team.

THE LAST TIME

62

17

THE LAST TIME

Anthony Ball

What I wouldn't give for some more memories with him
16th of December 2015
The shrilled voice.
She called my name through heightened fear.
Never could I be ready for those words my mother said next,
"I think we've lost him".
I raced down the stairs with absent breath and there he sat, slumped in his chair with a deep sleep disguise, his lips blue and his arms hanging limp by his side, a remote resting in an unclenched hand.
The TV continued to speak out loud, but he was no longer listening, his ears now attuned to the silence of the darkest void.
Then those three numbers, that call for help.
The phone call you never want to make.
The voice came through the telephone devoid of emotion that provided instructions.
So matter of fact… so removed from the horror and pain.
But I did as I was told.

With force pressed against his chest I desperately tried to restart his heart whilst mine was tragically breaking.
Wake up dad!! My repeating desire.
I've never wanted anything more in my life.
But I knew, I knew that his eyes would never look at me again, he would speak no more advice, laugh no more.
I had to watch as my mother wept from across the room, separated and isolated by a mass of bodies trying to bring back the dead.
What I wouldn't give for some more memories with him
It took time, too much time to close the chapter on this book of life.
The torture dragged on through the happy holidays
Waiting for Christmas to end and normality to return so that we could lay my father to rest.
Then that time came. The family's re assemblance
To see him again lying like a broken doll within a wooden box.
A face changed by unliving time that now bared only a resemblance to what it once was.
Skin resting loose from bone with clothes pulled over his rigid frame and his colour, faded like a sun-bleached magazine.
A haunting image that visits me still.
Not how I wanted to see him.
Only a squeeze of his foot could I manage as I said my last goodbye, before slipping away feeling just as lifeless.
What I wouldn't give for some more memories with him
I see him sometimes in dreams, he comes to me and hugs me. He looks just as I remember.
But it's not often enough.
In reality, I think I see him jogging down the street, that familiar figure like Homer Simpson...But then I know it's not him.
I look through the betting shop windows hoping to find him standing placing his bet.

Winning on the horses and smiling because of a 10 pence profit. It wasn't about the money; it was the joy of the win. I miss my dad.

Anthony J Ball is a new poet, writer and author from the West Midlands, and soon to be releasing a collection of poems and short stories in his first book, 'Asleep at 3 AM'.

THE LAST TIME

18

THE LAST TIME?

Lucy Onions

"Mum!" you say, clearly unimpressed by the fact I'm standing here, staring at you like a mad woman.

"Oh, okay," I say, knowing, deep down, that I need to leave you, that I'm cramping your style, "Just make sure you text me when you're on your way home please?"

"Yes, Mum," you nod, smiling at me.

I want to pull you into my arms and give you the biggest, squishiest hug, but I don't think you'll appreciate it, especially not now your friends are urging you to join them on the walk to school.

I turn away slowly, using every last nanosecond possible to take you in, to commit this moment to memory. Because this will be the last time. Not the last time of all the last times, but one of the hardest all the same.

I remember the day you were born, recall it as though it was yesterday morning. How long you were as they pulled you out of me, out of the "sunroof", not the usual way. What an entrance you made with your shock of thick, almost pitch-black hair (you'd never guess to look at it now) and those aqua blue eyes. The giggling and gurgling sound you made as the nurses gently placed you on the scales. Nine pounds four ounces of pure joy.

It's hard to forget those first few days, the emotional rollercoaster I was riding (cliché I know, but it's the only way to describe it). I adored you. I couldn't stand you. I couldn't take my eyes off you one minute, could barely look at you the next. I cried bucket loads for all those reasons. I'd never felt such deep exhaustion and pride in one go.

I fed you myself, waking you up every couple of hours, making written notes of the time and the length of the feed. I continued writing the diary I began when I found out I was pregnant with you. It was the only thing that kept me sane. Well, almost.

Once we got home everything seemed to settle. I was in my domain and you, and your Dad, were with me, and together, we could take on the world, one cluster-feed at a time!

The first last time happened four and a half months after. Your last feed was, in one way, heart-breaking, but in another way, a complete relief. It was your first 'I-don't-need-you-now-Mommy' moment. Your first little foray in independence.

Then there was the night you slept in you big-girls-bed for the very first time. The last time we whispered goodnight to you in your cot. The last time I rocked you to sleep.

Your first morning at nursery was the last time I had you at home, with me, all day. Leaving you with all those lovely ladies and lots of other children was as devastating as it was wonderful. It was then that I started to let go of you. I had to. But, Oh, the excitement in your little face when I collected you! The smile that stretched from ear to ear. For the first time, without being asked or persuaded, you ran to me, cuddled me. It wasn't to be the last.

Your first day in reception seemed to drag. It felt like forever and yet it flew by. They told me you got upset when you realised I wasn't collecting you before lunch and when I did arrive to pick you up, you ran to me, threw your arms around me. There was no beaming smile, not that day, but it came back, growing wider by the day, along with your confidence.

For the first time since you blazed comet-like into our world, I had time. Time for me. I felt guilty to begin with, felt bad for wanting to be apart from you, for wanting to do my own thing. We both needed our time away from one another and the conversations that came as a result of our daily separation were magical. Hearing and seeing you talk so excitedly about your day made me realise that everything, all of it, was so worth it.

For the first time ever, you asked how my day had been. I told you and you listened. Well, I think you did.

Over the next four years, there were many *firsts* and a few *lasts*, but none of us were entirely ready for your first residential trip away with school. Well, physically, we were, but emotionally – that's another story.

We held hands, me and your Dad, smiled at you as you headed off with your friends. You were full of it at first, a mix of bravado and excitement, but when you realised it was time to go, your resolve weakened, and you struggled not to cry, so we put on a united front. We smiled and told you everything was going to be okay, that you were only going to be away from home for a few days and that it would fly by. And we maintained our act, right until you walked through those doors, ready to embark on your first adventure without us. And we both put on our brave faces until we walked back home. That's when we let our guards down and had a bit of a cry. You were growing up, way too quick for our liking. We wanted to freeze time. We still do.

We always held hands, all the way to school, every day, since you were able and ready to walk there, and I remember the last time we used your pushchair. We had to set out of the house fifteen minutes earlier than normal to make sure you got to nursery before the gates were closed. That feels like an age away now.

Your first ever school disco may have only been an hour long, but when I collected you, you were red and sweaty from all the dancing and didn't stop talking all the way home. You were still chit-chatting about it when we shared your bedtime story.

Fast forward to just over six weeks ago; your very last, primary school disco. Fashions have changed a fair bit since your first, as has the music you listen to. We waited outside the gates for you rather than picking you up at the door, giving you the space and time to talk to your friends, to hug them, to cry.

And we cried too, the parents. We talked. We hugged. Because, just as you had your group of friends, some of them your best ones, so did we. We became best friends through you, our children. In another life, we never would have met and honestly, that's such a sad thought.

The last day of primary school came around all too quickly and the atmosphere was dense, heavy with sadness and mumbled goodbyes. It's quite a sight to behold, a playground full of crying children. Heart-breaking in fact.

School shirts and blouses were no longer the crisp, white articles they were when we left you that morning. Scribblings of every colour imaginable adorned backs, fronts, arms, collars and cuffs.

It was your last day with all your friends. Some you were destined to see again at high school, some you wouldn't.

And then that was it. Time to leave. Time to say goodbye. And it didn't matter one little bit that your friends were all around you when you ran up to me in the playground for a hug, a big, squishy one. You didn't care what anyone else thought when you broke down in tears because everyone was doing it – kids, parents and teachers alike. It was a last time for all of us.

You allowed me to walk you to the end of our street this morning. I say that, but you know as well as I that you wanted me with you as much as I needed to be with you.

Will it change you, "big school"? Will you develop an attitude? I really hope not. I hope that what we've taught you, how we've raised you, will stay with you always. Courtesy, manners and respect cost nothing.

You should be back by now. We timed the walk a few weeks back, and anyway, the school is only around the corner. Near enough, anyway.

You're just talking with your friends, that's all it is. Just chatting and walking. I need to calm myself down and get used to letting you go. After all, I've been doing that already, and I'll be doing it even more from now on, slowly but surely loosening my grip.

I hear the keys in the front door.

My heart soars.

I don't know what to expect.

Will you tell me everything?

Will you go straight to your room?

Will you run up to me for a hug, one of those big, squishy ones?

Or have we already had our last?

The seconds feel like hours.

Hurry up.

My stomach is churning.

The living room door opens, and…

"Hi, Mum. I'm back."

Yes. Yes, you are.

"Have you had a good day?" I ask her.
Silence.
Sniffles.
"I've really missed you," she replies.
Hug.

Lucy Onions hails from sunny Walsall in the West Midlands and runs a monthly book club at her local pub, The Homestead, called Walsall Book Social. As well as being a published author and writer, she fronts a twelve-piece Northern Soul and Motown band with her brother-in-law, Paul, called Soul'd Out UK. She's also a professional photographer, a handmade jewellery maker, and most importantly, a Mum. She's also proud to be one half of the publishing imprint that has produced this wonderful anthology, Black Dream. When she's not too busy (which isn't all that often), she likes to read, enjoy a good Shiraz or single malt (or both) and listen to her beloved records. She resides in Bentley with her husband, Simon, her daughter, Molly and a rather crazy Staffordshire Bull Terrier called Rosie.

https://www.facebook.com/LucyOnionsAuthor/

ABOUT THE PUBLISHER

James Josiah and Lucy Onions became great friends
through their shared love of books and music and met
years ago at a double book launch (of their own, self-
published novels, *C90* and *Shout the Call*) at their local,
independent bookshop. The rest, as they say, is history.

After years of proof reading and editing for others, as well
as for themselves, they decided to put their combined
experience in a hat, thus Black Dream (which is inspired
by a shared adoration of their favourite film, The Crow)
was born.

You can find out more about Black Dream here:
https://www.facebook.com/blackdreampublishing